iVy + bEAN

ALSO AVAILABLE:

IVY + BEAN AND THE GHOST THAT HAD TO GO
BOOK ❷

"Best mates Ivy and Bean reunite for some schoolyard hijinks. . . . This strong follow-up to Ivy + Bean is bound to please." —*Kirkus Reviews*

"This story defies expectations of what an early chapter book can be." —*School Library Journal*

IVY + BEAN BREAK THE FOSSIL RECORD
BOOK ❸

"This is a great chapter book for students who have recently crossed the independent reader bridge."
—*School Library Journal*

"Just right." —*Kirkus Reviews*

IVY + BEAN TAKE CARE OF THE BABYSITTER
BOOK ❹

"Early chapter-book readers will enjoy this."
—*School Library Journal*

IVY + BEAN BOUND TO BE BAD   BOOK ❺

iVy + bEAN

BOOK ❶

written by annie barrows + illustrated by sophie blackall

chronicle books · san francisco

For Clio, of course, but also for Claire, Keith, Maddy, Sam, Vincenzo, Melissa, Quinn, Chephren (and Jennifer Ennifer), Noah, Jonathan, Raejean, Dominic, Tanisha, Veronica, Christopher, Gabi, Xenia, Paul, and Amber —A. B.

For Olive and Eggy —S. B.

Text © 2006 by Annie Barrows.
Illustrations © 2006 by Sophie Blackall.

Book design by Sara Gillingham.
Typeset in Candida and Blockhead.
The illustrations in this book were rendered in Chinese ink.
Manufactured in China.

Library of Congress Cataloging-in-Publication Data
Barrows, Annie.
Ivy and Bean / by Annie Barrows ; illustrated by Sophie Blackall.
p. cm.
Summary: When seven-year-old Bean plays
a mean trick on her sister, she finds unexpected support
for her antics from Ivy, the new neighbor, who is less
boring than Bean first suspected.
ISBN-13: 978-0-8118-4903-6
[1. Friendship—Fiction. 2. Neighbors—Fiction.] I. Blackall, Sophie, ill. II. Title.
PZ7.B27576Ivy 2006
[E]—dc22
2005023944

10 9

Chronicle Books LLC
680 Second Street, San Francisco, California 94107

www.chroniclekids.com

CONTENTS

NO THANKS

Before Bean met Ivy, she didn't like her. Bean's mother was always saying that Bean should try playing with the new girl across the street. But Bean didn't want to.

"She's seven years old, just like you," said her mother. "And she seems like such a nice girl. You could be friends."

"I already have friends," said Bean. And that was true. Bean did have a lot of friends. But, really, she didn't want to play with Ivy because her mother was right—Ivy did seem like such a nice girl. Even from across the street she looked nice. But nice, Bean knew, is another word for boring.

Ivy sat nicely on her front steps. Bean zipped around her yard and yelled. Ivy had long, curly red hair pushed back with a sparkly headband. Bean's hair was black, and it only came to her chin because it got tangled if it was any longer. When Bean put on a headband, it fell off. Ivy wore a dress every day. Bean wore a dress when her mother made her. Ivy was always reading a big book. Bean never read big books. Reading made her jumpy.

Bean was sure that Ivy never stomped in puddles. She was sure that Ivy never smashed rocks to find gold.

She was sure that Ivy had never once in her whole life climbed a tree and fallen out. Bean got bored just looking at her.

So when her mother said she should play with Ivy, Bean just shook her head. "No thanks," she said.

"You could give it a try. You might like her," said Bean's mom.

"All aboard! Next train for Boring is leaving now!" yelled Bean.

Her mother frowned. "That's not very nice, Bean."

"I was nice. I said no thanks," said Bean. "I just don't want to. Okay?"

"Okay, okay." Her mother sighed. "Have it your way."

So for weeks and weeks, Bean didn't play with Ivy. But one day something happened that changed her mind.

BEAN HATCHES A PLAN

It all began because Bean was playing a trick on her older sister.

Bean's older sister was named Nancy. She was eleven. Nancy thought Bean was a pain and a pest. Bean thought Nancy was a booger-head. Ever since she turned eleven, Nancy had been acting like she was Bean's mother. She ordered Bean around in a grown-up voice: "Comb your hair." "No more pretzels." "Brush your teeth." "Say please."

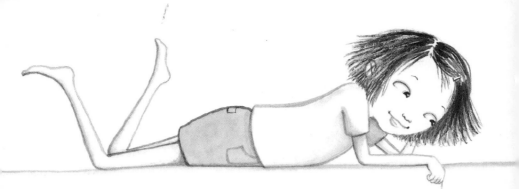

Bean's mother said that Nancy was going through a stage. Bean knew what that meant. That meant Nancy was bossy. Bean also knew that nobody likes bossy kids, so she was trying to help Nancy be done with her stage. Here's how she helped: She bugged Nancy until Nancy freaked out. Bean thought this was pretty helpful.

The afternoon that Bean got her great idea, she was shopping with her mom and Nancy.

Actually, Bean was
being dragged along
by her mom and
Nancy. Bean hated
shopping. Nancy loved,
loved, loved it.

Nancy was trying on skirts. Lots of skirts.
She put on a purple skirt. She looked at her
front in the mirror. Then she turned to the side.
Then she turned around and tried to look at
her behind.

"Looks good," said Bean. "Let's go."

"Be patient just a little longer, Bean," said
Bean's mother. "I think it's cute, honey," she
said to Nancy.

Nancy looked in the mirror some more.
"Do you think the pockets are dumb?"

"I like the pockets," said Bean's mom.

"Get it, get it, get it!" moaned Bean. She had never been so bored in her entire life. She was so bored she fell on the floor. Then she took a tiny peek up at the lady in the dressing room next door. *Yow.*

"Get up, Bean!" said her mother. "This minute."

Bean got up and sat on the triangle seat again. She waited. Nancy looked at herself.

"I kind of like it," Nancy said. "But it costs forty dollars. That's all my money. I could get two shirts for forty dollars."

"Don't be a tightwad," said Bean. She had just learned that word. It meant someone who didn't like to spend money.

"Don't call your sister a tightwad," said Bean's mom.

Bean saw Nancy's eyes looking at her in the mirror. "Tightwad," Bean mouthed without any sound. Nancy's eyes got narrow, and so quick that their mother didn't see, she stuck out her tongue. Then Nancy turned to their mother and said, "I think the skirt costs too much, Mom. I think I'd rather try on some tops."

Bean knew then that Nancy was being slow on purpose. Just to drive her crazy.

Bean thought about kicking her in the shin. But then she got the idea. It was a great idea. It was also a helpful idea, one that would teach Nancy not to be such a tightwad. And best of all, her idea would make Nancy freak out. "You'll be sorry," Bean mouthed to Nancy.

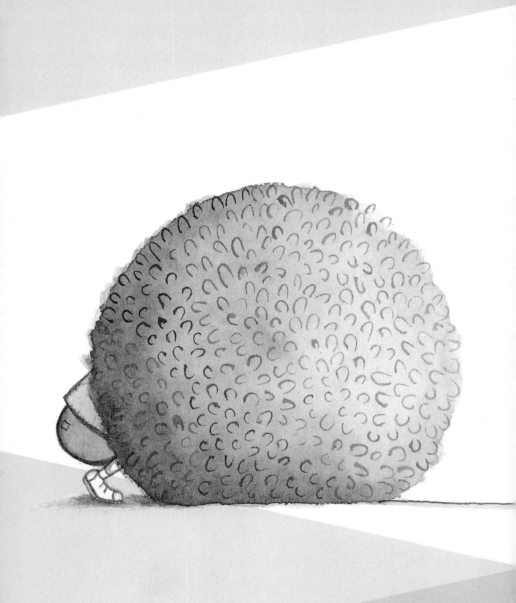

THE GHOST OF PANCAKE COURT

Bean was hiding inside a big, round bush in her front yard. The bush was right next to the sidewalk, and it was very scratchy and sticky inside, but Bean needed to be in the bush for her plan to work. Here's how Bean's plan went: She took a $20 bill out of Nancy's purse and taped a long thread to it. She put the $20 bill on the sidewalk. Then she held on to the other end of the thread and climbed into the bush. Nancy would be coming home from school soon. She would see the money on the sidewalk. She would bend down to pick it up. Bean would quickly pull the money away. And then Nancy would freak out. Bean could hardly wait.

There was only one problem. Nancy didn't come. Bean sat inside the bush for a long time. A branch poked her arm. Leaves fell down her shirt. She itched. She waited. Nothing happened. It was very quiet. Bean was hardly ever this quiet for this long. Because there was nothing else to do, she looked at the house across the street. Really, it wasn't across the street. It was around the street. Bean loved her street. The first reason was its name: Pancake Court. The second reason was that it ended in a big circle right in front of Bean's house. Her dad called it a cul-de-sac. Bean called it cool. If Bean started riding her bicycle at the end of the block and pedaled really, really hard, she could whiz around the circle, tilting low over the sidewalk like a motorcycle racer.

Slam! Bean looked up. She saw Ivy come out onto her front porch and plop down on the top step. Bean squinted at her. Ivy looked strange. She wasn't wearing a dress today. She was wearing a black bathrobe with lots of little pieces of paper stuck to it. Weird, thought Bean. She squinted some more. Instead of a big book, Ivy was carrying a stick, painted gold. Bean made a face. What a goony costume, she thought. What a dork.

Ivy sat. She didn't do anything. She just sat there all by herself. That was another strange thing about Ivy. She didn't mind being alone. She never played with anyone.

Bean played with *everyone.* Big kids, little kids, all the kids in the neighborhood played with Bean. Even crummy Matt—who was so crummy he threw other kids' toys into the road—wanted to play with Bean.

She took care of the little kids. When they fell down and got blood all over their knees, Bean would take them home to get Band-Aids. The big kids let her play with them because she had good ideas, like seeing how many backyards they could cross without touching the ground. Bean loved big groups of kids playing big games, like pirates or hide-and-seek.

Sometimes Bean wished she were an orphan so she could live in an orphanage with a hundred other kids. Of course, she didn't tell her mother and father that.

Bean watched Ivy, alone on her front porch. Wasn't she lonely? Now Ivy was muttering something that Bean couldn't hear. And then she began to wave the stick in the air. Bean couldn't stand it anymore.

"What the heck are you doing?" yelled Bean from inside her bush.

Ivy looked all around. Bean forgot that Ivy couldn't see her. "What's with the stick?" she yelled.

Ivy's eyes got big. "Who's there?" she said. "Are you a ghost?"

A ghost! What a great idea! Bean made her voice scratchy and spooky. "Yessss," she howled. "I am the ghost of Mr. Killop.

I lived in your house before. And I died there, too."

Mr. Killop had actually moved to Ohio, but Bean thought it was more interesting to say he had died. "I've come to haunt you! Tonight when you're sleeping, I'll wrap my icy fingers around your neck!"

"Bean! What are you yelling about?"

Oops. It was Nancy.

BEAN MEETS IVY

Bean peeked out between leaves. Nancy hadn't seen the $20 bill. She was standing on it. Hmm, thought Bean. Her plan was a bust, but if she kept on being a ghost, maybe she could scare Nancy a little. "I'm going to wrap my fingers around your neck, too," she howled in her spooky voice. "And I'm going to spit in your ear!"

"No, you're not," said Nancy. She didn't sound scared. She reached into the bush and yanked Bean out. "Stop yelling." That's when she saw the $20 bill. "Hey!" she said. "Where did you get the money? You don't have twenty dollars." Then she saw the string. "I see what you're doing, burp face! I bet this is my money, too!" Then she picked up the bill and looked at it. "You stole my money! I'm telling Mom!" She began to pull Bean toward the front door.

Uh-oh, thought Bean. None of her ideas were working out today. Now she had two choices. She could go inside with Nancy and face Mom. Or she could run.

So Bean fell over on the ground and started to wail. "My ankle! *Ow-wow-wow!* My ankle's killing me! It's sprained!" She held her ankle.

Nancy frowned. "You didn't sprain your ankle, you faker!" she said, but she bent down to take a look.

That was all Bean needed. She stood up and ran. She ran out of her yard and around Pancake Court until she found herself in front of Ivy's house.

"*Oooooh!* You're in trouble now, Bernice Blue!" yelled Nancy. "I'm going to tell Mom!" Bernice was Bean's real name. People used it only when they were yelling at her.

Bean couldn't help it. She just had to stick her tongue out and say, "*Pppppthbt!*" Then she just had to turn around and wiggle her behind at Nancy.

"That's it!" Nancy yelled. "I'm getting Mom!" She stormed into the house.

For a minute, Bean felt happy. She loved making Nancy mad. But when Nancy was gone, Bean began to worry. Mom hated it when she did more than one bad thing at a time. Bean counted: taking the money, lying about her ankle, leaving the yard without asking, and wiggling her behind at Nancy. Four things. Five if you counted pretending to be a ghost. Bean was going to be in big trouble. How big? No dessert, for sure. No videos for a week, maybe. But it could be even worse.

Her mom might send her to her room for the rest of the day. Bean hated that.

"Hide."

Bean looked up. She had forgotten all about Ivy. Ivy was still sitting on her porch. She had been watching the whole time. She knew that the ghost of Mr. Killop was really Bean inside the bush. Bean expected her to be mad. But she didn't look mad. She looked excited. "Hide," she said again.

Hmm, thought Bean. Maybe Boring Ivy was right. If her mom couldn't find her, she couldn't send her to her room. If she stayed out until dark, her parents would stop being mad and start being worried. Her mom might say, "Oh, my poor little Bean. My poor little baby!" Then they'd be so happy to see her when she came limping home that they probably wouldn't punish her at all. They might even let her have *seconds* on dessert.

That settled it.

"Okay," she said to Ivy. "Where?"

"Follow me."

Ivy came down the stairs and slipped behind a bush growing against her house. Bean followed her and crouched down under the wide leaves.

"No, get up. This is just the beginning," said Ivy. "I'm going to take you to a secret spot."

"This isn't it?" asked Bean. The bush looked pretty good to her.

"No. This is the passageway." Ivy pressed her back against the house and

edged along. Bean edged along, too, the wall scraping her back. They turned a corner and edged some more. Ivy's house was big.

"Halt!" said Ivy. Bean halted. "Now," said Ivy, "close your eyes, and I'll take you to the secret spot."

"What? How come I have to close my eyes?"

"Because it's a secret," said Ivy. "Duh."

Bean couldn't argue with that. Ivy looked like a wimp, but she didn't talk like one. Bean closed her eyes. She felt Ivy take her by the elbow, and together they went down some steps. A door opened. More steps. Cool, damp air blew in Bean's face. Then they went up some steps. Another door opened. They were outside again. Ivy was taking Bean through some tall grass. "Shhh!" said Ivy suddenly. Bean froze. "Crouch down!" said Ivy. Bean crouched. There was a silence. "Okay, you can get up now."

"What happened?" asked Bean.

"Spies," said Ivy.

Bean figured Ivy was probably making that up.

"Now you can open your eyes," Ivy said.

IVY HATCHES A PLAN

Bean opened her eyes. They were in a corner of Ivy's backyard. There was a big rock on one side and a small tree on the other. Between them was a perfectly round puddle. "This is the secret spot?" asked Bean. She had expected something more secret looking. Like a cave.

"Yes. They'll never find you here," said Ivy. "You can stay for as long as you want. I'll bring you food."

"But I only need to stay until dinner-
time," Bean said.

Ivy looked disappointed. "I thought
you wanted to run away."

"I do. But only till dinner."

"Oh."

Bean felt bad about not
staying. "Wouldn't you get in
trouble if your parents found
out I was living here?" she
asked.

"They don't come out here
much," Ivy said. "My mom is
afraid of ticks."

"You probably don't ever
get in trouble anyway," said
Bean, feeling glum. "I'm
always in trouble."

"I do too get in trouble," said Ivy.

"No, you don't," Bean said. "You read books all the time. You can't get in trouble for reading books."

Ivy said, "I will get in trouble— really huge trouble—if I do what I want to do. What I *plan* to do."

Bean waited. "Well? What do you plan to do?"

Ivy looked all around before she whispered, "Spells. Magic. Potions."

"Really? You mean like a witch?"

"Yes. Well. Not yet. But I'm going to be a witch," said Ivy. Her eyes were glowing. "I'm learning how."

Bean looked at Ivy's black bathrobe. It was kind of dirty now, and some of the little pieces of paper had fallen off. Bean saw that the papers were cut into star and moon shapes. Bean also saw that Ivy didn't know how to draw stars. Some of them had four points and some only had three. The moons didn't look so good either. "Is that a witch's robe?" she asked.

"Yeah," said Ivy.

"Did you make it yourself?" asked Bean.

"Yeah."

"It's nice," said Bean politely. It didn't look like a witch's robe. It looked goofy. "I didn't know you could learn to be a witch. I thought you just had to *be* one."

"That's what most people think," said Ivy. "But I'm learning. I probably know more than most born witches my age. I just learned this spell that makes you invisible."

"Wow." Bean could use that for sure. "Will you teach me? That would be great."

"I haven't done it yet," Ivy admitted. "You've got to have a dead frog."

"Oh."

"It would be really mean to kill a frog."

"Yeah."

"That's why I dug this pond." Ivy pointed to the puddle with her gold stick. "I'm hoping a frog will come here and die."

Bean didn't mention that it looked like a puddle. "Wow," she said. "What's the stick for?"

"That's my wand," said Ivy.

Bean couldn't help it. She burst out laughing. "That's not a wand. That's just a stick painted gold!"

"It is too a wand!" Now Ivy looked mad. "And you better watch out, or I'll use it on you!"

Bean stopped laughing. "Use it how?"

"I'll cast the dancing spell on you. You won't be able to stop dancing for the rest of your life. Like this." She started jumping up and down, kicking out her legs and waggling her arms.

"Could you really?" asked Bean.

Ivy stopped dancing. "Maybe. I was just going to test it when you started yelling about being a ghost."

"Who were you going to test it on?" asked Bean.

Ivy's face turned red. "Nobody," she said.

Bean could tell she was lying. "Come on. Who?"

Ivy's face got redder.

"Come on. Tell me!" said Bean.

Ivy looked at the dirt. "You," she said in a low voice.

"Me?!" yelped Bean. "What did I ever do to you?"

"I'm sorry," said Ivy. She did look sorry.

"That's okay," said Bean. There was a pause.

"My mother keeps on saying

what a nice girl you are," Ivy said. "She's always telling me I should play with you. It's driving me nuts."

Bean couldn't believe it. "That's what my mother says about you. That's so funny. But you're not nice at all! You're a witch!"

Ivy giggled. "You're not very nice either. You were doing that ghost thing in the bush."

Bean was embarrassed.

"The part about the icy fingers was good," said Ivy. "What were you doing in there, anyway?"

Bean sat down on the rock. "I was waiting for Nancy. That's my sister. She's a total pain in the kazoo. I put twenty dollars on a string, and I was going to pull it out of her hand when she reached down to pick it up."

Ivy nodded. "Is that why she got mad at you?"

"No. She got mad at me because it was her twenty dollars." Bean felt glum again.

Ivy saw that Bean was worrying. "Are you going to be in trouble?"

"Yeah. Probably. I'm not supposed to mess with her money." Bean thought. "You don't have a going-back-in-time spell, do you?"

"No. Those are hard," said Ivy. She looked at her pond. "I wish I had a dead frog."

"That would be good," said Bean. "But wait a second—what about the dancing spell? Could you put it on Nancy?"

"So she'll dance for the rest of her life? How is that going to get you out of trouble?" Ivy asked.

"It's not," said Bean. "But it would be really funny."

BEWARE

Once they had agreed to cast a spell on Nancy, Bean stared long and hard at Ivy's robe. Those little pieces of paper had to go. "The first thing we have to do is make you look more like a witch," she said.

Ivy looked down at her bathrobe. "Why?"

Bean tried to explain without hurting Ivy's feelings. "If you want other people to believe you're a witch, you have to look more witchy."

"But I don't care if other people believe me," said Ivy.

Bean shook her head. What a weird kid. "It'll make your spells better, too. You've got to dress for success." Her mother said that all the time. It usually meant that Bean had to put on a clean shirt. "Besides, it'll be fun. Do you have face paint?"

Ivy nodded. "In my room. Upstairs." She pointed to a window.

"Is your mom inside?" Bean asked.

"I guess," said Ivy.

"Is she going to tell my mom where I am?" Grown-ups stuck together that way. Bean's dad said it was because they were all in a club together, but Bean felt pretty sure he was making that up.

Ivy tapped her wand against her hand. "Maybe we should sneak in, just to be sure."

That was fine with Bean. She loved sneaking. She loved face paint, too. And she was really going to love watching Nancy kick her legs and wave her arms for the rest of her life.

They went in the back door to the kitchen. Bean could hear Ivy's mom talking on the telephone somewhere in the house.

"This is going to be easy," whispered Ivy. "She's working." She yelled loudly, "Hi, Mom! Can I have a banana?"

"Hang on a second," Bean heard Ivy's mom say. Then, to Ivy, she said, "Honey, I'm on the phone. Get your own banana." There was the sound of a door shutting.

"Okay!" yelled Ivy. She smiled at Bean. "See?"

Very tricky, thought Bean. Ivy was turning out to be a lot more interesting than she had expected.

They walked softly past Ivy's mom's door and up the stairs. They were very quiet. At the top of the stairs, there was a door with a sign that said "Beware" in red glitter glue letters. That was Ivy's room.

When she went in, Bean stood still and looked all around. "This is way,

way cool," she said. She had never seen a room like Ivy's. There were thick lines drawn on the floor, marking out five sections. Each section was like a different room. In one section, there was a small sofa on a rug and a bookcase stuffed with books. In another was a table covered with pens and paper and glitter glue and paint. Ivy's bed, with a canopy made of silver netting, was in another. A dresser and a folding screen painted with clouds were in the fourth section.

The fifth section had nothing in it except dolls. Bean had never seen so many dolls in her life. There were the regular plastic kind of dolls. There were the weird staring dolls with fancy costumes that were kept in glass cases at the toy store.

There were stiff wooden dolls. There were china dolls: small ones, smaller ones, and tiny ones. There was one doll that was really a rock dressed in clothes. All the dolls were seated around a doll-size blanket. Even the mushy baby dolls that couldn't sit by themselves had been propped up with blocks. In the middle of the blanket lay a Barbie doll, wrapped up in toilet paper. All the other dolls were watching her.

"Neat," said Bean. "A mummy."

"Yeah," said Ivy. "I'm going to build a pyramid to bury her in. As soon as I figure out how."

"I know how," said Bean. "Nancy made one out of sugar cubes last year. I can't believe your parents let you draw lines on your floor."

"It's only chalk," said Ivy. "It comes off. I change the lines when I change the rooms. For now, I'm thinking about getting rid of the dressing room and making it into a kitchen."

"Is that one the dressing room?" asked Bean, pointing to the section with the dresser and the folding screen.

"Yeah."

"I like the screen," said Bean, "but a kitchen is a little bit boring. Maybe you could turn it into a science lab for making potions. The screen could protect your secrets."

"A lab," said Ivy, thinking. "A witch's lab. That's a pretty good idea."

Bean looked over to the table with the paint and the glitter glue. "What's that room called?" she asked.

"That's my art studio," said Ivy.

"Cool," said Bean. "Let's fix up your wand."

In Ivy's art studio, there were plenty of sequins and jewels and streamers and pipe cleaners. First they wrapped the wand with silver pipe cleaners. Then Bean attached streamers to the end. Then Ivy put some stickers on. Then Bean put plain glue on the top and dipped it in a jar of glitter. She stuck a big red jewel on the top. The wand dripped a little, but it looked much, much more magic than it had before.

"Now," said Bean when that was done, "let's work on your robe."

"What's the matter with it?" asked Ivy.

"All the stars and moons are coming off. See?" Bean pointed. "It will look better if we draw them on with sparkly markers."

Ivy looked embarrassed. "I can't draw stars very well."

"I can," said Bean. "I'll teach you."

Bean showed Ivy how to draw dots for the star points, then connect the dots with lines. Ivy practiced on paper for a while, and then they stretched the bathrobe over the table and began drawing. Ivy's stars were a little bent, but they all had five points. Soon the black robe was covered with silver stars and gold moons.

Once that was done, Ivy got out her face paint. Bean couldn't believe it. The set had 24 colors. "Wow! Let's do green stripes," said Bean. "Or green dots." There were three different greens.

"No. Witches are only green in movies," said Ivy. "Real witches are just regular-colored."

"But you've got all this great face paint," said Bean. "We've got to use it for something."

Ivy thought. "You can put black around my eyes."

"Okay. But aren't real witches kind of pale, because they go out mostly at night?" asked Bean.

"I guess," said Ivy. "Kind of pale. But not green."

"My mom knew a guy who turned green. It was because he watched TV all the time," said Bean. But she could tell that she wasn't changing Ivy's mind. "What if we did all white, with black around your eyes?" she suggested.

"Yeah," Ivy nodded, "with a couple of blobs of red on my cheeks, for blood."

"That's good!" Bean agreed. "Blood is good!"

So Bean carefully smeared white all over Ivy's face except her lips. Then she drew red drops down her cheeks. They didn't really look like blood. They looked more like red tears, but that was a pretty scary thing, too. Then Bean drew thick black lines around Ivy's eyes. Both girls thought that witches' hats were dorky, so they wrapped Ivy's head in a black scarf (borrowed from her mother's dresser drawer). It looked almost like long black hair.

Ivy stared at herself in the dressing-room mirror. "Wow," she said. "I look really strange."

And she did.

EASY-PEASY

Now they were ready to begin. Ivy went to the bedroom section of her room and pulled a cardboard box out from under her bed. Then she looked at Bean. "This part is really secret," she said.

"I promise I won't tell anyone," said Bean.

Ivy opened the box and took out a square thing wrapped in pink silky cloth.

It was her spell book. Bean thought that a spell book would be mysterious looking, with a magic sign on the cover or something. But this spell book was plain black. It was old, though. Ivy said it was almost a hundred years old. The pages were yellowish.

"Where'd you get it?" Bean whispered.

"My aunt gave it to me," Ivy said.

"Is she one?" asked Bean.

"She says she isn't," said Ivy. "But I'm not so sure."

Ivy flipped through the book for the dancing spell. She read it to herself, and then she whispered it, but so low that Bean couldn't hear. Bean didn't mind. Everyone knew that witches' spells were private. After a few minutes, Ivy said, "Got it. It's a pretty easy spell. The only thing we need is worms."

Luckily, there were lots of worms in Bean's backyard. Tons. But now they were going to have to sneak into Bean's yard and dig them up. Without Nancy seeing.

But also luckily, Bean knew how to get into her yard by going through the other backyards on Pancake Court. There was

one really
gross dog-poopy
yard and there was
Mrs. Trantz, who didn't
like kids in her garden, and
there was a lot of climbing. But
aside from that, Bean said, it was
easy-peasy.

Ivy put the big black book in her backpack. Bean tucked the wand into her back pocket. It was still a little drippy, but there was nothing Bean could do about that. Carefully, they tiptoed down the stairs. Ivy's mother was still working in her office, and they slipped past her door like quiet ants. Soon they were moving quickly toward the back fence.

Ivy, Bean saw, did not really know how to climb a fence. She just jumped at it,

hoping that she would get to the top.
Bean showed her how to find the little
holes and bumps that make a ladder.

When they got to the top, Bean whispered, "This is Ruby and Trevor's house. They have a good sandbox."

The good news was that there was a gate on the other side of Ruby and Trevor's yard. The bad news was that it led to the really gross dog-poopy yard. Bean and Ivy walked on tiptoes, but still Ivy stepped in some. Fester, the dog whose poop it was, came out to sniff them. He was a nice dog, and he seemed sorry that his yard was so disgusting.

The next fence was low and easy, except that the wand fell out of Bean's pocket, and she had to go back and get it. Then came

Jake the Teenager's house. There was loud music with lots of bad words in it coming from the garage. There was no way

Jake the Teenager was ever going to hear them walking through his backyard.

Mrs. Trantz was next. Getting into her yard was no problem. Ivy and Bean climbed over the stone wall and dropped down onto her lawn. Everything in Mrs. Trantz's yard was perfectly neat. Her tulips were lined up in rows. Her apple tree was tied so that its branches grew flat. Her birdbath had no birds in it.

"If Mrs. Trantz sees us, she's going to be really mad," said Bean. Bean knew this garden. It was very long, and there was no way to go around it.

"Is she going to throw rocks at us?" asked Ivy. She looked a little scared.

"No. She just talks, but it's worse than throwing rocks." Bean sighed. "Maybe she's not home."

But Mrs. Trantz was home. They were halfway across her perfect yard when she came outside. She stood on her patio and glared at them. "Bernice," she said in a high voice. "Come here."

Bean took a few steps toward the patio.

"Closer, please, Bernice. It seems that we need to have another one of our little talks."

Ivy came and stood beside Bean next to the patio.

"Who are you?" said Mrs. Trantz, frowning at Ivy's white witch face.

"My name is Ivy," said Ivy.

"Well, Ivy, children are not allowed in my garden. Maybe you can teach your friend Bernice that." Mrs. Trantz gave a short, dry laugh. "Because Bernice does not seem to be able to remember it by herself. Do you, Bernice?"

"I remember, Mrs. Trantz, but it was just sort of an emergency," said Bean. "I'm sorry."

Usually when you say you're sorry, people say something nice back to you. Not Mrs. Trantz. She said, "I don't think you're sorry, Bernice. If you were sorry, you wouldn't keep coming into my garden when I have asked you not to. Do I need to call your mother again?" She smiled in an unfriendly way.

Bean heard Ivy sucking in her breath. She's about to do something, thought Bean.

"I'm going to throw up," Ivy said loudly.

Yuck! thought Bean, whirling around to see. Ivy looked at her and crossed one eye a tiny bit. Bean looked closely at Ivy. Then she said, "That's the emergency I was telling you about, Mrs. Trantz."

Mrs. Trantz looked worried.

Ivy burped. It sounded horrible.

Mrs. Trantz jumped back. "Go! Go home! Run!"

"That's what we were trying to do, Mrs. Trantz," Bean said sweetly. She was having a good time watching Mrs. Trantz's face.

"Go! Now!" yelled Mrs. Trantz.

Ivy gagged.

Mrs. Trantz ran inside her house and looked at them through a window. She waggled her hand to shoo them away.

"We'll be going now, Mrs. Trantz!" called Bean.

She waved good-bye as she and Ivy walked away. Ivy gave one more disgusting burp, just for fun. Bean tried to hold her laughs in, but they came out her nose. And then Ivy couldn't hold her laughs in either. It was a good thing they were in the next yard by then.

It really was easy-peasy after that. They went across Kalia's yard. Kalia was in her high chair at the kitchen window. She waved her spoon at Bean. Bean waved back and then put her finger to her lips. "Shhh," she whispered.

Finally they came to Bean's own yard.

BEAN'S BACKYARD

"You peek over. See if Nancy's there," said Bean. "She might be in the yard looking for me."

Ivy nodded and stood up. She could just see over the fence. "I don't see anyone," she said.

"Then they're probably out looking for me," said Bean. She pictured her mom and Nancy with worried faces. "I've been gone for a long time."

"Let's go get the worms," said Ivy, pulling herself over the fence.

Bean's backyard was a big rectangle. There was a nice part, with flowers and neat grass. And then there was a messy part,

with lumpy grass and a
trampoline and a playhouse
that Bean had had since
she was little. She could
barely fit inside it anymore.

There was stuff lying all over the messy part: hula hoops, balls, arrows, shovels, buckets, and a broken stilt (Bean had really hurt herself that time). The worms were in the messy part, over next to the playhouse, where the ground was wet.

Ivy and Bean grabbed shovels and a bucket and got to work. At first, there was just a lot of mud. Then there was mud and a few worms. But the more they dug, the more worms they found. Six. Ten. Thirteen worms. The worms oozed and curled through the mud. Bean liked the way they were fat one second and stretched out and skinny the next. She and Ivy dug deeper and deeper, until they had made a big muddy pit in the ground. It was almost two feet across, and water dribbled down the sides. Worms were squirming at the bottom of the pit, trying to get away. Bean felt a little sorry for them. But Ivy just picked them up and dumped them into the bucket. Bean thought of Nancy kicking and waggling, and she began dumping them into the bucket, too.

"How many do we need?" asked Bean. The worms were piled on top of one another on the bottom of the bucket.

Ivy looked "Only ten. But the more worms we have, the harder she'll dance."

"This is enough," said Bean. "Poor worms."

"All right," said Ivy. She looked toward Bean's house. "Let's go see if your sister is home."

"Okay, but we'd better sneak," said Bean.

Bean's house was good for sneaking. At the back, there was a porch. If you crawled like a bug across the porch, you could look through a big window into the kitchen.

The girls ran toward the bushes that grew next to Bean's porch and ducked down, hiding. Quietly, they began to creep up the stairs that led to the porch. Very quietly, they crawled across the floor. And then—Bean heard a sound.

She froze.

There it was again.

A sob.

It was someone crying. Bean listened.

It sounded like Nancy.

Bean put her hand on Ivy's arm and pointed to the window. They crawled to it and peered in like spies.

There was Nancy. She was sitting at the kitchen table. She was alone. She was crying.

Bean got a funny feeling. Nancy was usually so bossy, so nosy, so sure she was right. It was weird to see her cry, all alone.

"Maybe she's crying because she thinks you're lost," whispered Ivy. "That's kind of nice."

Bean didn't answer. She had never thought she could make Nancy cry. Bean felt a lump in her throat. She remembered that Nancy let her snuggle into her bed when she had bad dreams about the spooky man. She remembered that Nancy let her play with her glass animals some-times, even after she had broken the starfish.

She remembered that Nancy had once bought her a fairy coloring book with her own money. Bean looked at the tears rolling down Nancy's cheeks. Poor Nancy. Bean  sniffed. Maybe she didn't want to put the dancing spell on her sister, after all.

Nancy said something. Bean couldn't hear it, but she was sure it was something about missing her.

"What?" said Bean's mother's voice from another room.

"Everybody has them!" Nancy shouted. "Everybody but me! I'm the only one who has to wait!" She began to cry harder.

What? Bean pressed her face against the window.

Her mother's voice said, "We've talked about this a million times. You can have them when you're twelve."

"Even some of stupid Bean's friends have them!" yelled Nancy.

Suddenly Bean knew what Nancy was crying about. "She's not sad about me at all! She's crying about pierced ears!"

hissed Bean to Ivy. Bean got mad. Really mad. She was even madder than she had been when Nancy tried to drag her into the house. Bean was so mad she forgot all about being sneaky. She stood up and banged on the window with her fist. "You're a big turkey!" she yelled.

Nancy stared and then jumped up. "Hey! Hey! Mom! Bean's back! Get in here, Bean breath!" She flashed out the back door before Bean could even begin to run. In two seconds flat, she had Bean by the arm and was pulling her in the door. "Just wait till Mom gets hold of you," she was saying. "You're going to be in so, so, so much trouble—"

"STOP!" yelled Ivy. She stood in front of Nancy, waving the wand at her face. "I command you to free Bean!"

THE SPELL

Nancy stopped dragging Bean across the porch and looked at Ivy. "Who are you?" she asked.

Ivy smiled and slitted her eyes. With her white face and red blood drops, she looked very witchy. "It matters not. Free my friend," she hissed.

Wow, thought Bean. She's really going for it.

Nancy dropped Bean's arm and lifted one eyebrow, which was something she had just learned how to do and did all the time. "What's that supposed to be?" she asked in a snippy, grown-up way, looking at Ivy's wand.

Ivy shook the wand in Nancy's face. "This is your doom," she said in a deep voice.

"It's a wand," said Bean, looking back and forth between Ivy and Nancy. She was beginning to worry. Maybe Ivy was going for it too much. With older sisters, you had to be able to say that you never meant what you said, that you were kidding the whole time. Ivy didn't seem to know that.

Nancy snorted. "It's a *stick*," she said. She looked at Ivy's robe and giggled. "Nice bathrobe, too. You guys are complete and total dweebs."

Uh-oh. Bean looked at Ivy. Her cheeks were red under the white paint, and her eyes glittered. She looked like she might cry.

Suddenly, Bean was furious. Before, she had been really mad. But now Nancy was making fun of Ivy, and that made Bean furious.

Without even stopping to think about it, Bean reached down into the bucket she was still carrying. She got a big handful of pink worms. For a second, they squiggled in her hand. And then she threw them at Nancy's face.

Some of them fell onto Nancy's shirt. Some of them got stuck in her hair. But one landed on her eyebrow and wiggled there, trying to find some dirt.

Nancy was so surprised she froze. She just stood with her mouth hanging open, staring at Bean.

Calmly, Bean reached into the bucket again and got another handful of worms. She aimed better this time. She got one in Nancy's mouth.

"Phoo!" The pink worm went flying as Nancy spit it out. There was a tiny moment of quiet, and then she opened her mouth wide and let out a giant scream.

Bean and Ivy looked at each other and smiled. "Whatever happens next," their eyes said, "that was worth it." And then they began to run.

Nancy tore after them, still screaming. Bean zigzagged across the lawn because she knew it was harder to catch someone who was zigzagging. Ivy zigzagged, too, right behind Bean.

"Worms! Worms!" Nancy was screaming. She had lost her mind. *"Ahhhhhh!"*

Bean could hear her mother calling, "What on earth?! Girls! Girls!" Bean and Ivy ran around the trampoline, with Nancy close behind. They jumped over the hula hoops and the stilt and headed for the trees. Nancy followed, still screaming. She was right behind them. She was so close she could almost grab the soft folds of Ivy's robe—she was just about to get it.

"Help!" squealed Ivy. Bean gave a yank and pulled the robe away in the nick of time.

Ivy and Bean swerved for the playhouse. Maybe they could get inside it before Nancy tackled them.

"Come on!" Bean yelled. Together they jumped over the worm pit, squeezed into the playhouse, and slammed the door. "Whew!" they said together.

Then it happened.

Nancy was still chasing them.

She was running toward the playhouse.

And toward the worm pit.

The big, muddy worm pit.

Bean and Ivy knew it was there.

But Nancy didn't. And she didn't see it.

She charged toward the playhouse, and—
whoops!—her foot landed on the side of the
muddy pit. Ivy and Bean looked out the
playhouse window, and they saw Nancy
skidding on the slimy edge of the hole.

Back and forth she wobbled, trying to keep her balance. She kicked out one foot. She waved her arms wildly. She kicked out her other foot. She waved. She kicked.

It was perfect.

"She's dancing!" yelled Bean.

"The spell worked!" yelled Ivy.

And just at that moment, with a sloppy, gloopy thud, Nancy slipped off the edge and landed in the muddy goo at the bottom of the worm pit.

NO DESSERT

"No dessert," said Bean. "No videos for a week. But at least they didn't make me stay in my room."

Ivy was sitting next to Bean on her front porch. It was almost dark. They watched the bugs flying around the streetlight.

"I don't think they're really mad," said Ivy.

"You don't?" They had seemed pretty mad to Bean.

"They have to act mad so they'll seem fair to your sister," Ivy said. "But your mom had this little, teeny smile on her face when she pulled Nancy out of the pit. She thought it was funny."

Bean smiled, too, remembering. "It *was* funny."

"It was great."

"Nancy says she's never going to speak to either of us ever again. And she took back the coloring book she gave me."

"Well, she never spoke to me before today, so that won't be any different for me."

"It'll be better for me. But I bet she doesn't stick to it." Bean yawned. It had been a big day. She turned to Ivy. "Do you think the spell is what made her dance?"

"Of course." Ivy sounded very sure. But after a minute she said, "I didn't have time to say the spell, really. I just sort of thought it at the last second."

Bean stared into the shadowy yard. "Maybe that's why she didn't dance for very long—because you only thought the spell instead of saying it."

"Next time I'll say it."

"You're going to do it again? On who?" Bean asked.

"I was thinking about that Mrs. Trantz," said Ivy.

Bean pictured Mrs. Trantz kicking up her feet on the edge of a muddy pit. It would be a beautiful sight. "Can you teach me to burp like that?" asked Bean.

"Sure," Ivy said. "Maybe I'll try something new on Mrs. Trantz. Like a storm of grasshoppers."

"Is that a hard one?"

"No, but we have to start with a lot of grasshoppers," said Ivy.

"It seems like all the spells have bugs in them," said Bean.

"Not all of them," said Ivy. "Potions don't."

Potions. That sounded fun. "Let's make a potion," Bean said.

"Okay," Ivy said. "Tomorrow we'll make potions."

"I know what," said Bean. "Tomorrow let's fix up a lab in your room. Then we can make potions." She pictured a lab with shelves full of little bottles. She and Ivy would wear goggles.

Ivy sat up straighter. "Yeah! That'll be good. We'll dump the dressing room and get some shelves. Shelves with little bottles. And maybe a counter."

"Bean?" Bean's mother came out onto the front porch. "There you are. It's almost bath time. Ivy, do you want me to walk you home?"

"Okay," said Ivy.

But Bean's mom sat down beside Bean and looked at the nighttime sky. "You girls have certainly had a big day, haven't you?"

Bean leaned against her mother's arm. "Tomorrow we're going to make a lab in Ivy's room."

"You are, are you?" said Bean's mom. "What for?"

"Potions," said Ivy.

"What kind of potions?" asked Bean's mom.

"Secret potions," said Ivy.

There was a silence. Then Bean's mom said, "No matches. No poison. No explosions. No deadly fumes. No bugging Nancy. Is that clear?"

Ivy and Bean looked at each other and rolled their eyes. "Weren't you the one who was always telling me to play with her?" said Bean. "Wasn't this all your idea in the first place?"

Bean's mother smiled at them in the dark.

The light on Ivy's porch came on, and Ivy's mom stepped out the door. She waved across the street. "Time to come in, honey." Down the stairs and across the circle she came in the moonlight.

Ivy stood up.

So did Bean.

"See you tomorrow."

"See you tomorrow."

And the day after that, Bean added in her mind.

Ivy, holding her mother's hand in the middle of street, turned around to look at Bean. "And the day after that," she said.

ivy + bean

BOOK 2

One, two, three, four, five, six, seven, eight, nine, ten—*thud*. Bean crashed into the grass.

"Ouch," said Ivy, looking up from her sandwich. "Doesn't that hurt?"

"No. I'm just dizzy," said Bean. She sat up, and the playground began to tilt. Ugh. She lay down again.

Now Emma stood up. She lifted her arms above her head, took a big breath, and began. She did nine good cartwheels before she fell on her head.

Ivy had eaten a hole in the center of her sandwich. She looked through it at Emma. "Are you all right?"

"Sort of," said Emma.

Now it was Zuzu's turn. Zuzu was the best cartwheeler in the Gymnastics Club. She was also the best backbender. She could do seven round-offs in a row. Nobody else could do even one.

Zuzu pulled down her ruffled pink shirt and raised her arms. One, two, three, four, five, six, seven, eight, nine, ten, eleven, twelve cartwheels, and still Zuzu landed on her feet. Then, she arched over backward. She flung her arms over her head and made a perfect backbend. She looked like a turned-over pink teacup. Then she rose back up—*boing*—like a doll with elastic in its legs.

"Wow," said Ivy.

Bean jumped up. "Twelve cartwheels or bust!" she said.

"Wait," said Zuzu. "What about Ivy? Aren't you going to do a cartwheel, Ivy?"

"I'm guarding the jackets," said Ivy.

"But Ivy, this is the Gymnastics Club," said Zuzu. "You can't just guard jackets."

Why not? Ivy wondered.

"We'll teach you how if you don't know," said Emma.

"She knows," said Bean. "She can do a cartwheel. I've seen her."

Ivy looked at Bean in surprise. Why was she saying that? Ivy had never done a cartwheel in her life. Ivy put her sandwich down next to Emma's jacket.

"There's just one little problem," she began.

"Hey Leo!" yelled Bean, "If I get clobbered, I'm going to tell the Yard Duty!" Leo was the head of the soccer kids.

"It's not even near you!" yelled Leo. He was right. The ball was on the other side of the field, near MacAdam, a weird kid who sat under the trees and ate dirt when he thought no one was looking.

"Okay!" yelled Bean, feeling lame. She had only been trying to help Ivy.

"There's just one little problem," Ivy said again. "We've got an emergency situation going on. Right over there." She pointed.

Emma, Zuzu, and Bean followed Ivy's pointing finger across the playground. She was pointing directly to the girls' bathroom. The one right outside their classroom.